W9-BJK-409

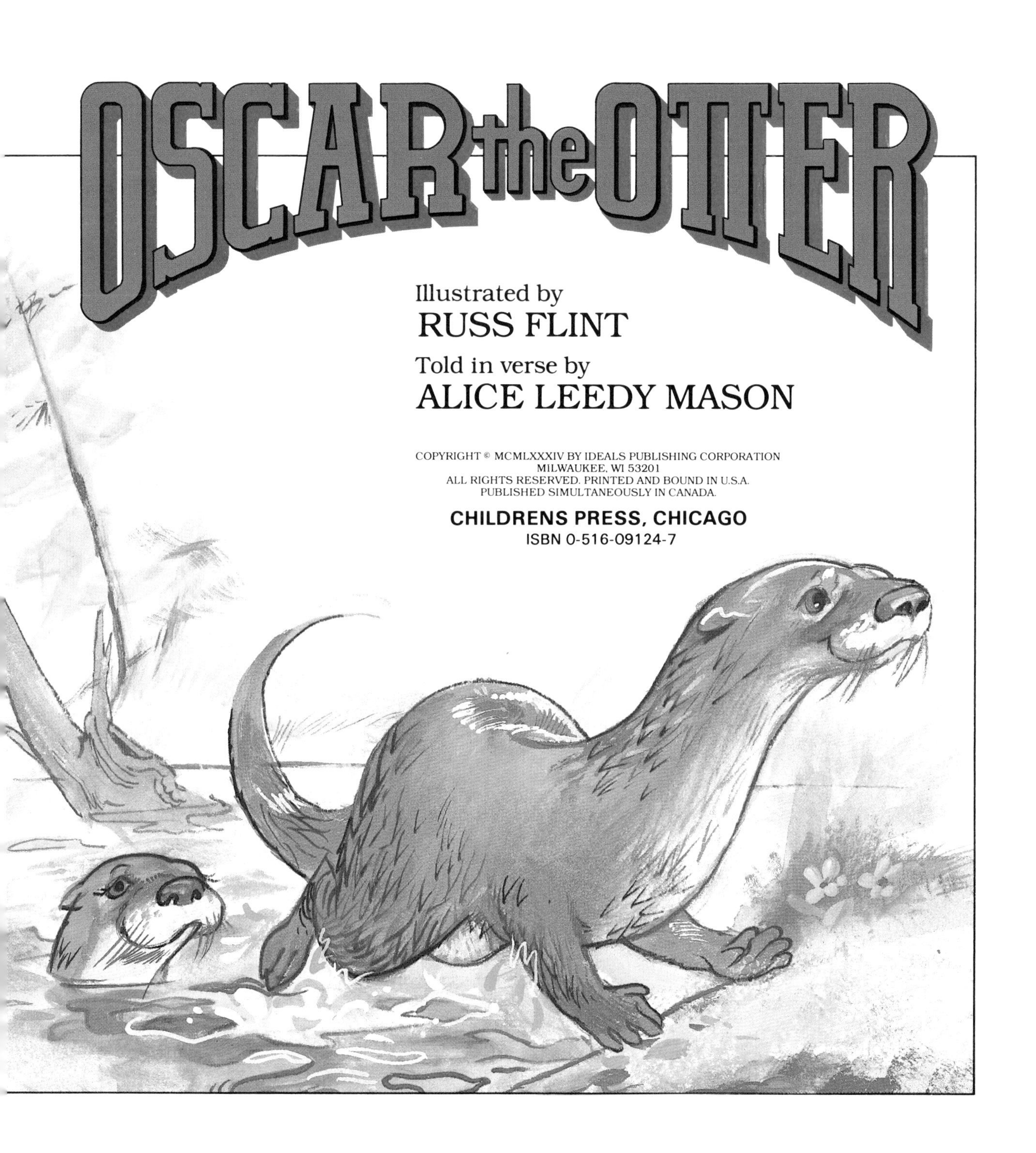

OSCAR the OTTER

Illustrated by
RUSS FLINT

Told in verse by
ALICE LEEDY MASON

CHILDRENS PRESS, CHICAGO
ISBN 0-516-09124-7

Oscar the Otter
lived down by the river
Learning of life in the sun.
From morning till night
He found much delight
In sliding and splashing for fun.

But Oscar was far from contented.
He dreamed of a new kind of play
And of old-timer's tales
Of ships large as whales...
He wished he could go far away.

He was dreaming of travel and fortune
When his cousin, Olivia, cried,
"There's nothing to do.
I'm bored through and through!
Let's adventure! Do things we've not tried!"

They left when the su
was just risin
They slid down each slic
they could fin

Oscar romped through the day,
Moving farther away;
Thoughts of home
never entered his mind.

It's exciting!" Olivia whispered.
"The next otters we meet may seem strange.
We may like them a lot,
Or else we may not!
We may find ourselves wanting to change."

The cousins at noon met new otters,
Who offered no friendship, no food.
Oscar said, "In our den
We invite strangers in.
But these otters aren't friendly —
they're RUDE!"

I thought that I wanted to travel
And maybe I'll try it someday.
Right now I'm for sharing,
For loving and caring.
I'm sorry that I ran away!"

As he spoke, Olivia pictured
Their families loving and warm,
Sharing food, having fun,
Feeling close to each one,
The den keeping all safe from harm.

A sudden loud clap of thunder!
Dark clouds threatened, crowding the sky...
Raindrops hurled down,
Lightning flashed all around!
Olivia started to cry.

Someone will help,"
Oscar promised.
They searched out a nearby den.
But, "No room in here!
Our family lives near,
And we've just enough room for our kin."

Just at the edge of the swampland
Oscar found a deep hole safe from rain.
"We can wait out the storm.
Rest here, dry and warm,
And tomorrow we'll head home again!"

Both families ran out
to greet them.
Their smiles were delightful to see!

Oscar said, "Now I know
What has always been so...
Home is the best place to be!"

Folks who've traveled far and free
Find home is where they want to be.